Princess

2000

stickers

Pretty, sparkly, friendly, and fun!

PaRragon

Bath • New York • Singapore • Hong Kong • Cologne • Delhi
Melbourne • Amsterdam • Johannesburg • Shenzhen

Princess Picnic Party

You're invited to a princess tea party! Fill this
pretty picture with more sandwiches, cakes, and drinks.

Use your stickers to give each teddy bear a tiara!

Princess tip: A princess is kind to animals as well as people!

Choosing Shoes

Which line leads Princess Polly to her missing shoe?

Puzzling Pile

Draw lines to match the pairs of princess shoes and boots.

Now find and circle four princess purses.

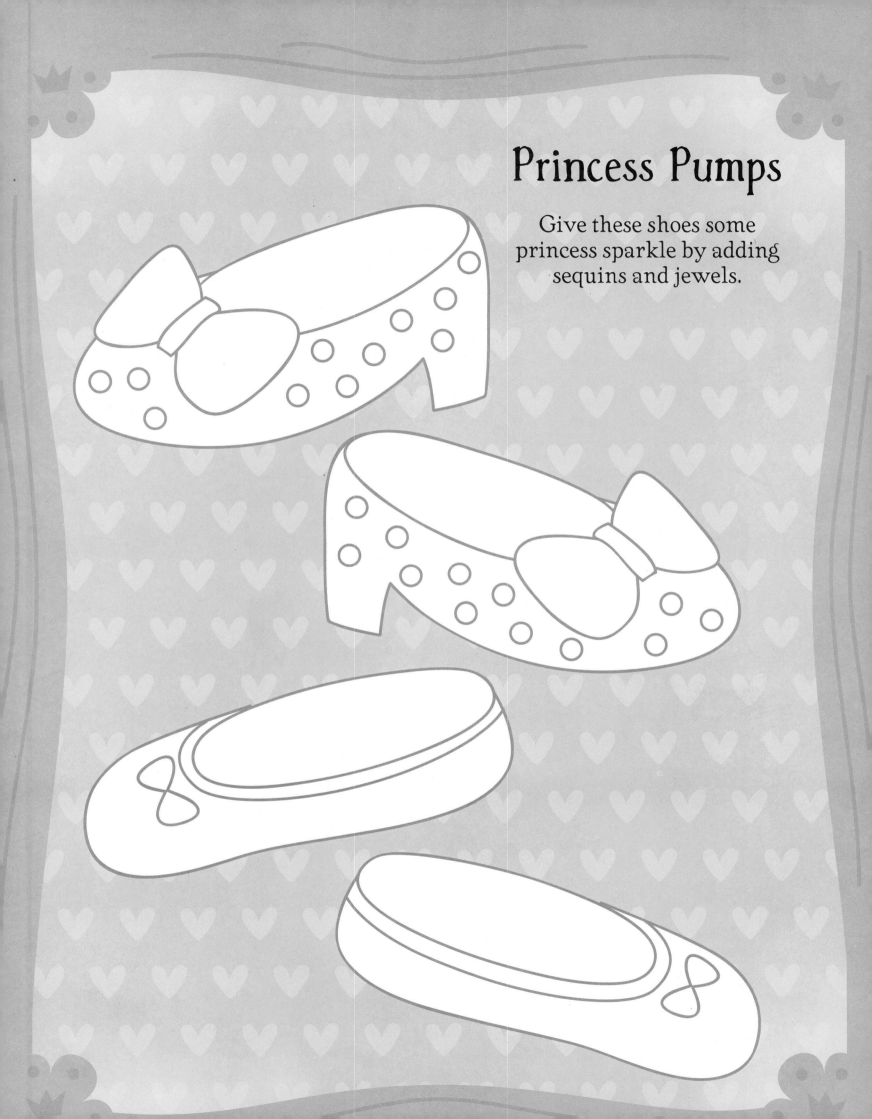

Princess Pumps

Give these shoes some princess sparkle by adding sequins and jewels.

Party Princess

Every princess loves to spin, twirl, and dance with her friends. But this ballroom is bare! Fill it up with decorations and princess guests.

Princess tip: A princess is friendly and welcoming!

Princess Playtime

Can you help Princess Rose
find her way through
the maze to her friends
in the middle?

Flutter-by Butterfly

Find and circle five differences between these utterly fluttery pictures.

Sparkly Shadows

Princesses come in all shapes and sizes. Some are tall and some are short. Match each princess to her shadow.

A   B   C   D

1   2   3   4

Palace Kitchen

These sweet-toothed princesses love to help out in the kitchen. Add cupcakes and treats of your own!

Decorate the cakes!

Princess tip: Princesses gladly help others!

Secret Shoppers

There are five princesses in this picture.
Can you find and circle them all?

Fashion Favorites

Princesses love matching accessories!
Color in these shoes to match these bags.

One of these tiaras is not like the rest. Can you spot the odd one out?

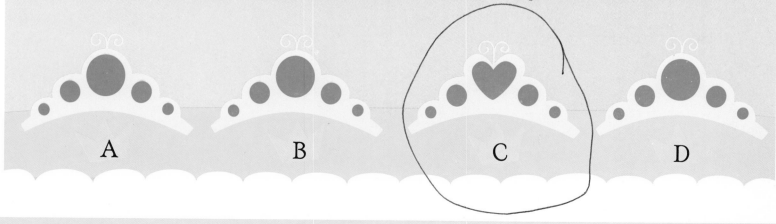

A B C D

Flower Fair

Add more flowers to the stalls and more princesses enjoying the palace garden flower show.

Color these roses in your favorite colors.

Count the daisies.

Princess tip: A princess loves pretty flowers!

Princess Painting

Are you ready to draw
Princess Daisy's portrait?
Make her as pretty as you can!

Picture Perfect

What a princess-perfect picture! Connect the dots to find out what this arty princess is painting.

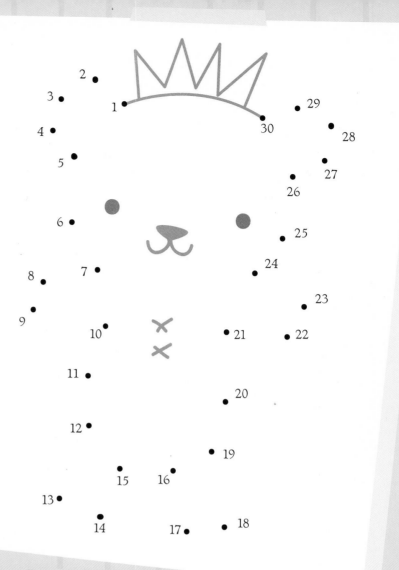

Painted Paws

Uh-oh! Which pet's paws have been in the paint pots?

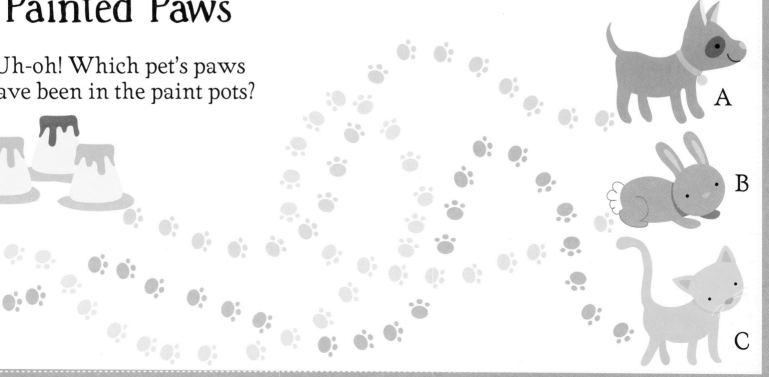

A

B

C

Princess Sleepover

It's time for a princess slumber party!
Add more princesses and toys for them to play with.

Princess tip: A princess likes to have fun with her friends!

Princess Brunch

There are five differences between these two pictures. Can you find them all?

Princess Puzzle

Help this princess complete the puzzle. Find and circle the last jigsaw piece.

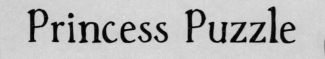 

Rainy Day Fun

It's raining outside, so the princesses are playing hide-and-seek! Can you find three princesses hiding?

Missing Jewelry

Uh-oh! The princesses have been playing dressing up and have lost the royal jewels!

Find and circle:
1 diamond necklace
2 sapphire bracelets
3 ruby rings

Princess tip: Princesses love dressing up!

How many tiaras can you count?

How many bags can you count?

Use your stickers to add
more gems and jewels!

Pretty Ponies

Color in the saddles,
reins, and leg warmers.
Then dress the ponies up
in jewels, ribbons, and tiaras!

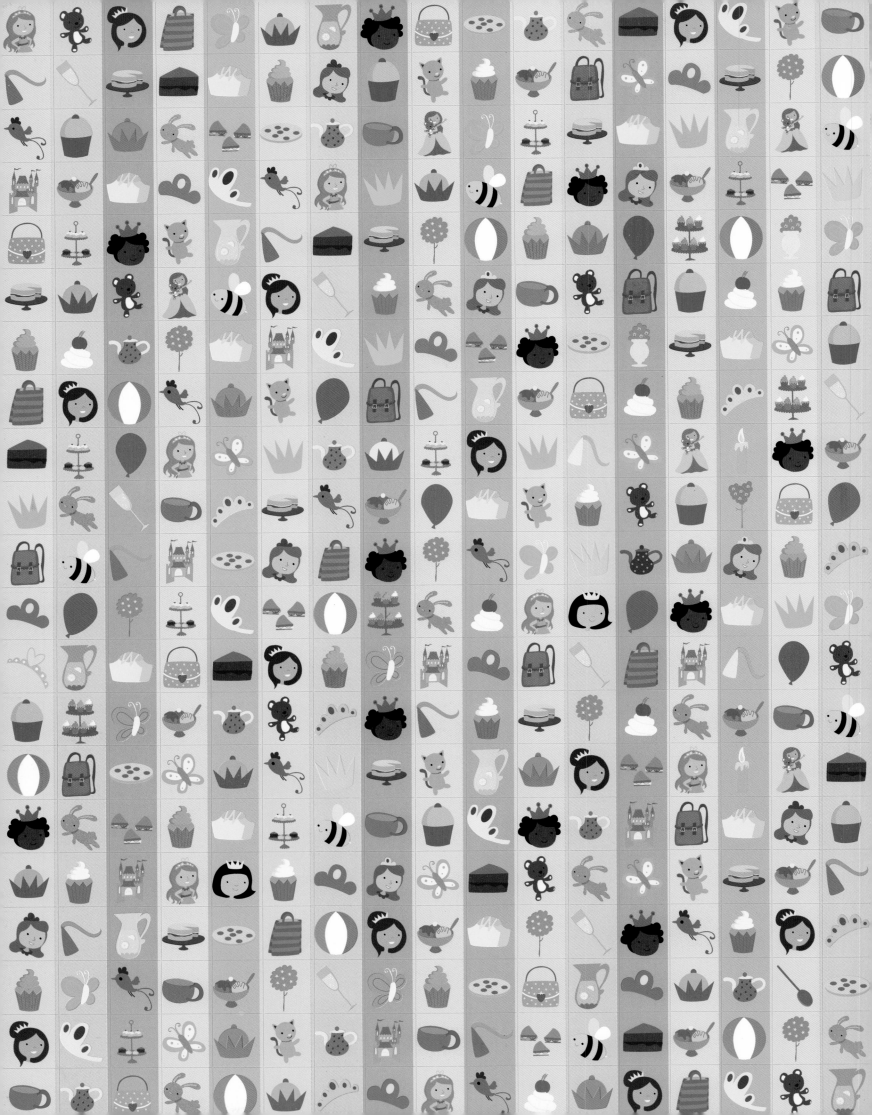

Pony Path

Which trail of hoofprints leads
Princess Poppy to the royal stables?

Pony Pairing

Only one of these shadows matches this pony
exactly. Circle the matching shadow.

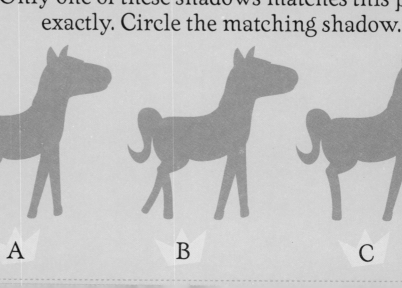

A   B   C

Princess Playground

Yippee, it's playtime! Fill the playground with swinging, skipping, and scooting princesses.

Princess tip: A real princess plays happily with others!

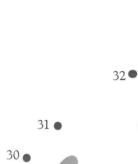

Princess Diary

What has Princess Daisy
drawn in her diary?
Connect the dots to find out!

33 ●   ● 1

35 ●

34 ●

32 ●   ● 2

31 ●

5 ●

30 ●   4 ●

6 ●

29 ●   26 ●

3 ●

7 ●

28 ●   27 ●

10 ●

25 ●   22 ●   9 ●

8 ●

21 ●   18 ●

17 ●   14 ●

13 ●

Now color
the picture.

24 ●   23 ●

20 ●   19 ●

16 ●   15 ●   12 ●   11 ●

Make this your very own princess diary page.
Draw a pretty picture of yourself dressed as a princess.

Write your
name here.

Circle the animal
you like the best.

Ballerina Princess

Look at these pretty princesses leaping and twirling!
Fill this ballet classroom with more ballerina
princesses learning to dance.

Princess tip: A true princess always tries her best!

Princess Packing

Sun, sand, and sea! Princess Lily is going on a beach vacation.
Circle five things to pack, then draw them in the suitcase.

Don't forget to add shoes and tiaras, too!

Princess Pairs

Which sun hat
matches this one exactly?

A

B

C

Jet-setting Princess

There are five differences between these jet-setting princess pictures.
Can you find them all?

Fluttering Friends

Princesses love beautiful butterflies!
Fill the palace gardens with more princesses
and their fluttering friends.

How many butterflies can you count?

How many bunnies can you count?

How many unicorns can you count?

Princess tip: A princess never moans or complains!

Royal Banquet

It's the night of a royal family dinner, and you are the chef! What yummy food will you add to this banquet table?

Banquets and Balls

These princesses love dressing up
for royal banquets and balls!
Color their dresses and shoes
in your favorite colors.

Splish Splash!

The princesses are learning how to swim!
Use your stickers to give them armbands and inner tubes.

Add more princess
swimmers in the pool.

Princess tip: Princesses like to learn new things!

Playful Puppies

Oops! Princess Lola has forgotten
to wipe her puppy's paws!
Follow the trail of muddy
paw prints to find out
where he is hiding.

Puppies in the Park

There are five differences between these two pictures.
Can you find them all?

Puppy Pairing

Only one of these shadows matches this puppy
exactly. Circle the matching shadow.

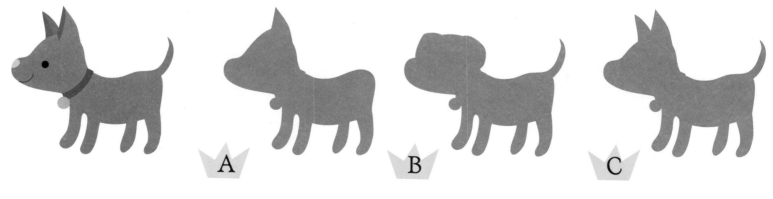

A

B

C

Princess Library

Princesses love reading books—especially fairy tales!
Fill the room with more books for these princesses to read.

Princess tip: Princesses enjoy reading and writing!

Princess School

Welcome to Princess School, where young princesses from far and wide are taught! Connect the dots to find out what this class is learning today.

Classroom Line

Which princess has brought her pet in for show-and-tell?

A   B   C   D

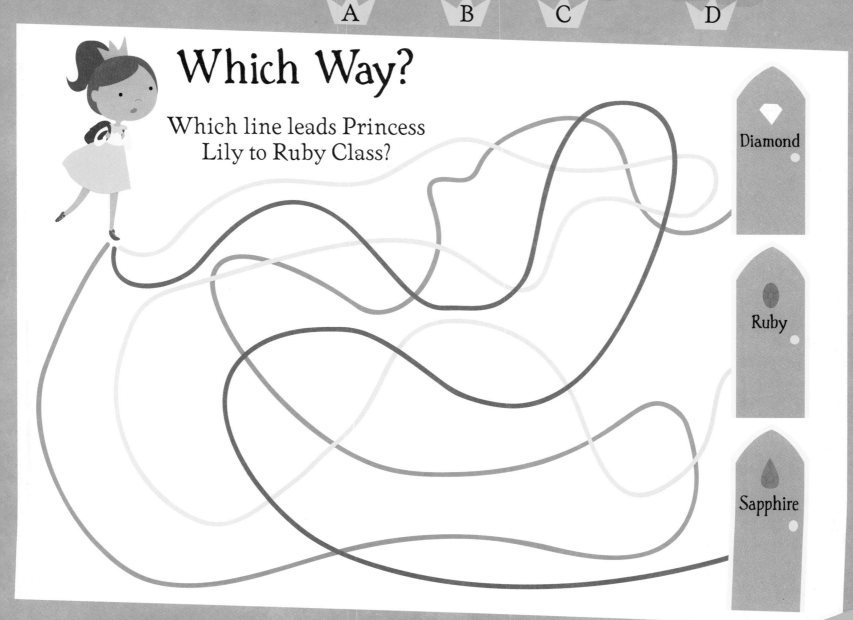

Which Way?

Which line leads Princess Lily to Ruby Class?

Diamond

Ruby

Sapphire

Princess Ponies

Fill these royal stables with
prize ponies and their proud owners!

Princess tip: Princesses enjoy taking care of animals!

Answers

Page 4
The pink line leads Princess Polly to her missing shoe.

Page 8

Page 9

A2, B3, C1, D4

Page 12

Page 13
C is the odd one out.

Page 17

Pet A's paws have been in the cans of paint.

Page 20

Piece A is the last jigsaw piece.

Page 21

Pages 22-23

There are 9 tiaras and 4 bags.

Page 25
The trail of yellow hoofprints leads Princess Poppy to the royal stables.
Shadow B matches the pony exactly.

Page 28

Page 33
A matches the sun hat exactly.

Pages 34-35
There are 10 butterflies, 3 bunnies, and 3 unicorns.

Page 41

Shadow C matches the puppy exactly.

Page 44

Page 45
Princess A has brought her pet in for show-and-tell.
The blue line leads Princess Lily to Ruby Class.